Bear
Sees
COLOURS

Karma Wilson

Illustrations by
Jane Chapman

SIMON AND SCHUSTER • London New York Sydney Toronto New Delhi

Mouse and Bear are walking;
they are chitter-chatter-talking.
So much for them to do.
And the bear

sees . . .

blue!

Blue flowers
by the trail.
Blue berries.
Blue pail.

Blue, blue EVERYWHERE!
Can you spy blue with Bear?

Along the trail hops Hare.
"Howdy-ho there, Mouse and Bear!"
Hare points up ahead.
And the bear

sees . . .

red!

Red blossoms.
Red cherries.
Red, juicy
raspberries.

Red, red EVERYWHERE!
Can you spy red with Bear?

Badger's at the pond
with his old wellies on.
"Look there!" Badger bellows.
And the bear
sees . . .

yellow!

Drippy, sticky,
oh-so-yummy
honeycombs
with yellow honey.

Yellow, yellow EVERYWHERE!
Can you find yellow, just like Bear?

Gopher's out with Mole.
They are on a little stroll.
Bear spots them by the stream,
and the bear

sees . . .

green!

Green mint
for making tea.
Green and sweet
tasty peas.

Green, green EVERYWHERE!
Can you spy green with Bear?

Raven, Owl and Wren
lay a picnic in the glen.
The friends all gather round,
and the friends

see . . .

brown!

Chocolate cake,
brown and sweet.
Brown cookies,
such a treat.

Brown eyes,
brown hair.
Friendly, fluffy,
brown . . .

BEAR!

Colours, colours EVERYWHERE!
Can you find colours, just like Bear?

To Emma. Bear and I say thanks.
—K. W.

To Jo, Jeremy, and Charlotte.
—J. C.

SIMON AND SCHUSTER • First published in Great Britain in 2014 by Simon and Schuster UK Ltd • 1st Floor, 222 Gray's Inn Road, London WC1X 8HB • A CBS company • Originally published by Margaret K. McElderry Books, an imprint of Simon and Schuster Children's Publishing Division, New York • Text copyright © 2014 Karma Wilson • Illustrations copyright © 2014 Jane Chapman • The right of Karma Wilson and Jane Chapman to be identified as the author and illustrator of this work has been asserted by them in accordance with the Copyright, Designs and Patents Act, 1988 • All rights reserved, including the right of reproduction in whole or in part in any form • A CIP catalogue record for this book is available from the British Library upon request • ISBN: 978-1-4711-2324-5 • Printed in China • 10 9 8 7 6 5 4 3 2 1 • www.simonandschuster.co.uk